Co

Written by Jack Gabolinscy

Cockroaches live
all over the world.
Some are very big and
some are little.

Cockroaches can be
different colours.
They can be brown, black,
blue, red, yellow, or green.

lizard

Many animals can
eat cockroaches.
Lizards like to eat them.
Birds, snakes, frogs, mice, and
rats can eat cockroaches.

spider

cockroach

Spiders like
to eat cockroaches, too.

A cockroach is an insect.
It has six legs and big eyes.
It can see lots of ways
at the same time.

eye

It is hard to catch
a cockroach.
When it sees you coming,
it runs away very fast.

A cockroach has its skeleton
on the outside of its body.
If you squash the cockroach,
its skeleton will go **crunch!**

When a cockroach gets big,
its skeleton can be too small.
So the cockroach grows
a new skeleton.
When you see a white cockroach,
it has just got a new skeleton.

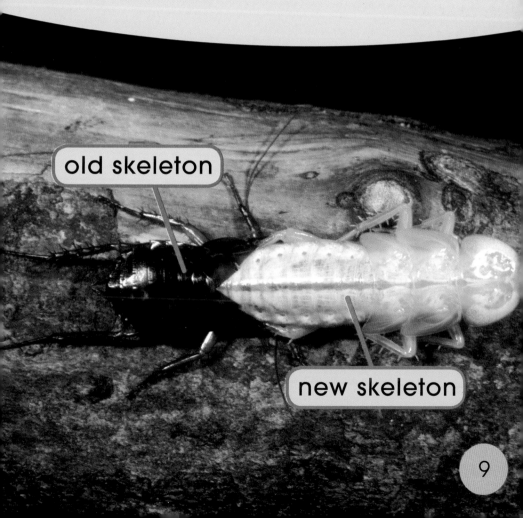

old skeleton

new skeleton

Cockroaches come out
to look for food at night.
They can climb up pipes.
They eat any food
they can find.

They get dirt on their legs.
Then they walk over food.
Yuck!

Cockroaches are pests.
They get germs
all over food and
then people eat it.
Sometimes they get sick!

People spray
the cockroaches,
but they can come back.
It is very hard to
get rid of cockroaches.

This cockroach was alive when the dinosaurs were here.

The cockroach is one
of the oldest animals
in the world.
It lived on Earth when
the dinosaurs were here!

Index

animals that eat cockroaches . 4-5

cockroach

    eyes 6

    legs 6

    skeletons 8-9

cockroaches

    and dinosaurs. 14

    and people. 12-13

food for cockroaches 10-11

getting rid of cockroaches 13

what cockroaches look like . . . .

. . . . 2-3, 6

where cockroaches live 2

Guide Notes

Title: Cockroaches
Stage: Early (4) – Green

Genre: Non-fiction
Approach: Guided Reading
Processes: Thinking Critically, Exploring Language, Processing Information
Written and Visual Focus: Photographs (static images), Labels, Caption, Index
Word Count: 233

THINKING CRITICALLY
(sample questions)
- Look at the front cover and the title. Ask the children what they know about cockroaches.
- Look at the title and read it to the children.
- Focus the children's attention on the index. Ask: "What are you going to find out about in this book?"
- If you want to find out about a cockroach's skeleton, what pages would you look on?
- If you want to find out about how people get rid of cockroaches, what page would you look on?
- Look at page 10. Why do you think the cockroaches look for food at night?

EXPLORING LANGUAGE

Terminology
Title, cover, photographs, author, photographers

Vocabulary
Interest words: cockroaches, pipes, skeleton, insect, lizards
High-frequency words: any, sometimes
Positional words: over, on, up, outside
Compound words: outside, sometimes

Print Conventions
Capital letter for sentence beginnings, full stops, commas, exclamation marks